The Muddily-Puddily Show

By Valerie Tripp
Illustrated by Thu Thai

✮ American Girl®

Published by American Girl Publishing

16 17 18 19 20 21 22 LEO 10 9 8 7 6 5 4 3 2 1

Editorial Development: Jodi Goldberg and Jennifer Hirsch
Art Direction and Design: Riley Wilkinson and Jessica Annoye
Production: Jeannette Bailey, Mary Makarushka, Cynthia Stiles, and Kristi Tabrizi
Vignettes on pages 90–93 by Flavia Conley

americangirl.com/service

For Jodi Goldberg,
with love and thanks

Meet the WellieWishers

The WellieWishers are a group of fun-loving girls who each have the same big, bright wish: to be a good friend. They love to play in a large and leafy backyard garden cared for by Willa's Aunt Miranda.

Ashlyn

Willa

Emerson

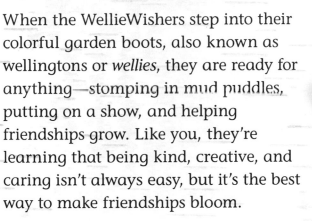

When the WellieWishers step into their colorful garden boots, also known as wellingtons or *wellies*, they are ready for anything—stomping in mud puddles, putting on a show, and helping friendships grow. Like you, they're learning that being kind, creative, and caring isn't always easy, but it's the best way to make friendships bloom.

Camille

Kendall

GARDEN MAP

Carrot's
🌸 Hutch 🌸

Playhouse

Garden
🌼 Gate 🌼

Aunt Miranda's
🌸 House 🌸

Garden Theater
🌸 Stage 🌸

Pond

N
W · E
S

Garden
❀ Shed ❀

❀ Tea Table ❀

❀ Veggie
Garden ❀

Chapter 1

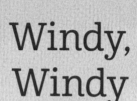

Windy, Windy

Swooooshhh! A playful wind pushed against Emerson's back. It blew so hard that she flew along, hurrying to meet her friends, the WellieWishers.

Emerson grinned. She loved the wind. The wind liked to stir up excitement and so did she.

9

Emerson liked the wind so much
that she made up a windy poem:

> Windy, windy blue-sky day,
> Swirl me up and blow me away.
> Lift me like a leaf or a kite
> Over the treetops,
> Up out of sight.

"Come on, Emerson," called
Camille. "Hurry up! It's your turn!"

"My turn to what?" asked
Emerson.

"You'll see!" said
Camille cheerfully.

"Oh, boy!" said Emerson. "I love jumping into leaves. Here I come!"

Ya-hoo! Emerson flew forward, took a flying leap, and landed—*floop*—face-first on her stomach in the big pile of leaves.

"Hooray!" her friends cheered, laughing at Emerson's face-first

landing. "Ya-hoo!" they hooted as they all ran and jumped and landed—*floop*—by Emerson in the leaf pile. The wind caught the scattered leaves and sent them flying up, up, up into the bright blue sky.

Emerson rolled over onto her back and—*swoosh!*—tossed handfuls of leaves up into the air. "Listen to my poem," she said.

Windy, windy
blue-sky day,
Swirl me up and blow me away.
Lift me like a leaf or a kite
Over the treetops,
Up out of sight.

"You're really good at making up poems, Emerson," said Ashlyn.

"Thanks!" said Emerson breezily. "It's easy."

"Don't you just love fall?" sighed Kendall.

"Yes!" said all the girls as they decorated themselves, putting leaves in their hair and their buttonholes and their pockets and their wellies.

"Come on," said Willa. "I brought apples for everyone. Let's go eat them under that pretty tree."

"Oh," gasped the girls.

"Look at this tree," said Willa. "Isn't it beautiful?"

"I *love* it! It's *won*derful," sighed Emerson.

"The leaves are *so* yellow!" said Camille.

Yellow as
the sun,

Yellow as the
butter on a hot,
toasty bun!

Yellow as a
ripe banana,

"Listen to us," laughed Kendall. "I guess Emerson was right—poetry is easy. Without even *trying,* we made up a poem about fall."

Suddenly, Emerson jumped up. "Oh, oh, *oh,*" she said, exploding with excitement. "I have just had the most *won*derful idea. You'll *love* it. Come on!"

Chapter 2

Fall for Fall

The girls stampeded behind Emerson. She ran to the garden theater and leapt up onto the empty stage.

"We," said Emerson dramatically, "are going to put on a show."

"A show!" echoed the girls.

"Our show will be called 'Fall for Fall.' It will be about all the things that make us fall in love with fall," said

Emerson. "Like the
whooshing wind—"

"And jumping
into a leaf pile,"
Camille added.

"And a whole tree
full of yellow leaves,"
Willa said softly.

"What will we *do* in the show?" asked Kendall.

"We've already got two good poems to recite," said Camille. She counted them on her fingers. "There's Emerson's 'Windy, Windy' poem, and the 'As Yellow As' poem we all made up."

"Will that be enough for a whole show?" asked Ashlyn.

"Well," said Emerson, "we'll also sing songs and dance dances—"

"Sing and dance?" asked Willa faintly. "All of us? Do we have to?"

But Emerson didn't hear her. Emerson was saying, "We'll sing and dance about fallish things, like ducks flying south for the winter, and pumpkins—"

"And splishy, splashy, muddily, puddily rainy days," suggested Camille.

"Do we *know* any songs or dances about fallish things?" asked Kendall.

"We'll make them up!" said Emerson with airy confidence.

"How will we do that?" asked Ashlyn.

Emerson stood in the middle of the stage, and a shaft of sunlight shone on her like a spotlight. She thought for a moment, and then she said, "Here's a song already." Emerson danced and waved her arms like wind-tossed branches. She fluttered her fingers like falling leaves. To the tune of "London Bridge Is Falling Down," she sang:

Autumn leaves are falling down,
falling down, falling down.
Autumn leaves are falling down,
Oh, so pretty!

Ashlyn jumped up onto the stage next to Emerson. Pulling the leaves out of her pockets and tossing them into the air, she sang:

> *Take some leaves and toss them up,*
> *toss them up, toss them up.*
> *Take some leaves and toss them up,*
> *Oh, so pretty!*

"That's good!" said Camille and Willa, clapping.

"That's *great*," said Kendall. "This is going to be the best show ever!"

Chapter 3

Fun
Work

The WellieWishers were bubbly with excitement and happiness when they met in the playhouse the next day.

"Let's practice our 'Autumn Leaves Are Falling Down' dance," said Ashlyn. She spun so that her tiara sparkled in the light as she sang, *"Autumn leaves are falling down."*

"Oh, that is so good," praised
Emerson. "And singing and dancing
are only part of the fun of putting on
a show."

Emerson rose up on her toes in happy excitement. "A show is like a party," she said. "You don't just go straight to eating the cupcakes. Before that, you have all the fun of planning and preparing and working to get ready."

"Working?" asked Camille.

"Oh, don't worry," said Emerson. "It's fun work. I gave each of you a job that you'll love, because it's doing what you like to do best."

"What's my job?" Ashlyn asked eagerly.

"You always make such pretty

party invitations," said Emerson.
"So your job will be making a poster
to invite people to the show." She
handed Ashlyn poster paper, pens
and markers, paint and paintbrushes,
glitter glue, and foil stars.

"Oh, good!" said Ashlyn. "That
will be fun for me." She looked very
pleased.

"And Camille," said Emerson, "you love dress-up, so you are in charge of costumes."

"Costumes!" gushed Camille. She was so excited that she dove into Aunt Miranda's trunk and began flinging things out. Shawls and shoes, caps and capes, robes and raincoats, belts and boots, gowns and galoshes, and fine, fancy feathers flew all over the room.

"What will I do?" asked Kendall.

"You like to build things," said Emerson. "Would you like to make the set?"

"Yes, I would. Very much," said Kendall. She flipped open her notepad to a blank page and started to draw right away.

"Willa, you are going to love your job," Emerson said. "Will you collect all the props we need, like fallen leaves, acorns, and pinecones?"

"Yes!" said Willa, nodding. She
took the big basket from Emerson and
sprinted out the door.

All of the WellieWishers were happily hard at work—except Emerson.

"Oh, dear!" said Kendall. "You gave all of us great jobs, but what about you, Emerson? I'm afraid you didn't save any fun work for yourself."

"Me?" said Emerson. "I'll make up more songs and dances and teach them to the rest of you."

"Do you have ideas for more songs and dances?" asked Ashlyn, looking up from her painting.

"Well," said Emerson, "I thought of a muddily-puddily song. Maybe we could dress up as ducks when we sing it."

"Oh, please sing it for us now," said Camille, rising from a sea of costumes.

"Okay," said Emerson. The girls watched as Emerson danced like a waddling duck and sang to the tune of "Row, Row, Row Your Boat":

> *Rain, rain, rainy day,*
> *Splishy-sploshy wet!*
> *Muddily, puddily, muddily, puddily,*
> *We love rain, you bet!*

47

Everyone was quiet for a second. Then Willa said, "Emerson, you've done it again. That muddily-puddily song is really good."

"And it's very funny the way you dance like a duck!" chortled Ashlyn.

Then all the WellieWishers burst out cheering, "Hooray for Emerson! Hooray! Hooray!"

Lucky
Duck

As yellow as some butter, as yellow as a bun—no, I mean a pear," Camille recited as she tried to juggle the foods in the poem. "As yellow as a lemon. Wait, maybe it's a banana?" *Ploop*, fruit fell at her feet. "Oh, I give up!" she said. "I get the words mixed up, and hold up the wrong thing, and then the rhyme isn't right, and—"

"Stop!" said Emerson. "I've thought of a better way to do it."

"What?" asked her friends. They looked worried. They were supposed to put on their show the next day, but Emerson kept coming up with changes. Great new songs and great new ideas just seemed to pop out of Emerson like popcorn from a popcorn popper. But Emerson had so many new ideas that the girls were getting confused.

"Ashlyn will stand behind you in her pumpkin costume and read the poem," Emerson said to Camille. "Then you just have to hold up the yellow thing that she names. That will be easier."

Ashlyn spoke up. Her voice sounded muffled inside the pumpkin costume. "But I can't read the poem because I can't see out of this pumpkin. I can't dance in it, either, because I can't see my feet. And it's hot and uncomfortable. Maybe I shouldn't wear the costume."

"No, no, you have to wear it!" said Emerson. "It'll be okay—you won't need to dance. Willa can do the muddily-puddily song and dance by herself."

"Me?" squeaked Willa. "By myself? I thought we were all going to be dressed as ducks and sing and dance with Ashlyn, the dancing pumpkin."

"Well, I only had time to make one duck mask," said Emerson, "so you're the only duck, you lucky duck."

"Oh, no," moaned Willa, who did not feel lucky at all.

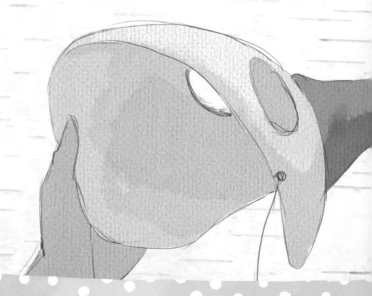

Willa put on the duck mask. She folded her legs under her and tucked her arms like wings behind her. She sat very still.

"Are you a duck laying an egg?" asked Kendall.

Willa shook her head. "I'm just thinking about flying south for the winter," she explained.

"No, no, no, we need *action*," said Emerson. "A *thinking* duck is boring. Fly—like this." Emerson flitted around the stage dramatically, moving her arms up and down, like big wings. "And then land like this." Emerson slid gracefully to the floor of the stage, like a duck swooping down and gliding onto a pond. "And then sing the muddily-puddily song."

Willa tried to fly gracefully like Emerson, but when she landed, she plonked down so hard that tears pricked her eyes. "I can't do it like you do it, Emerson," she said in a wobbly voice.

Emerson sighed. "All right, all right," she said. "Just sing the muddily-puddily song, then."

Willa shook her head. "I can't sing all alone," she whispered.

"Don't worry, you'll be fine," said Emerson.

"No, I won't," said Willa.

"Willa, is there something else you'd rather do in the show?" asked Camille.

"I could talk about pinecones," said Willa, perking up a bit. "I could tell how pinecones fall off trees in the late summer, or early fall, when they are big enough. There are male pinecones and female pinecones. The female ones are bigger and more prickly. When pinecones decompose—"

Emerson interrupted. "I don't think anyone is that interested in pinecones, really," she said.

63

Willa got all pink in the face.

"Maybe you could help me with the set, Willa," said Kendall quickly. "You can help me figure out how to have wind blow and leaves fly and rain fall."

"You mean you haven't figured that out yet?" asked Emerson. "When *will* you figure it out?"

Kendall frowned. "I don't know," she said, sounding as prickly as a pinecone. "I don't even know if I can do it. It may be impossible."

"Impossible?" Emerson repeated. "Impossible?" She clutched her head

with both hands and wailed, "I'll tell you what's impossible: putting on a show with all of YOU! Maybe we just shouldn't do the show at all."

Everyone was quiet. It was an awkward, uncomfortable kind of quiet. No one wanted to say anything for fear of making Emerson storm off in a huff. They were sorry to see her so frustrated and upset. But they were upset, too.

Willa felt hurt.

Kendall felt unappreciated.

Ashlyn felt confused.

Camille felt sad to see her friends unhappy with one another. She said gently, "Let's take a break from rehearsing."

"Okay," the girls mumbled glumly. They followed Camille into the playhouse.

Chapter 5

Listen

It was quiet inside the playhouse. Willa and Ashlyn washed the paintbrushes. Kendall picked up paper scraps. Emerson helped Camille pick up costumes and put them away.

As Camille put a scarf back into Aunt Miranda's trunk, she began— very, very softly—to whistle "Row, Row, Row Your Boat."

Ashlyn picked up the tune. Just as softly, she sang, *"Rain, rain, rainy day..."*

Willa joined her, singing almost in a whisper, *"Splishy-sploshy wet..."*

Then Kendall chimed in, and all four girls sang quietly, *"Muddily, puddily, muddily, puddily. We love rain, you bet."*

When the song was finished, the four girls smiled at one another.

"That's really a good song, Emerson," said Ashlyn.

"Hmph," sniffed Emerson. "If it's so good, then why won't Willa sing it?"

Camille put her arm around Willa. "Willa," she said, "just tell Emerson how you feel. And Emerson, you need to listen, okay?"

Willa said softly, "Emerson, you are really good at singing and dancing. But being in front of people is hard for me. I don't want to be on the stage all by myself." She shuddered. "It gives me a case of the willies just to think about it." She gave a small smile. "Willa's willies, get it?"

"Walk in Willa's wellies and get a case of Willa's willies," Kendall joked gently. She looked at Emerson. "I have

something to tell you, too. I want to
make the rain and wind and falling
leaves that you asked for, but I'm
not sure I can, and I don't think you
understand how hard I'm trying."

71

"I'm trying, too," Camille piped up. "But I get confused when you keep changing things, Emerson. All of your ideas are great, but I can't keep them straight. It's like those bananas and pears and lemons in the poem. I get them all mixed up, like a fruit salad!"

"My problem is my pumpkin costume," said Ashlyn. "I can't see out of it, and it's hot and uncomfortable. And I don't like being hidden away inside the pumpkin. I feel as if I'm not in the show at all. But you told me I had to wear it."

Emerson swallowed
hard. She took a
shuddery breath,
picked up her
little round suitcase,
and then, without
saying a word,
she left.

73

Chapter 6

Emerson Acts Up

A little while later, the girls saw something in the doorway. It was an enormous clown shoe, waving back and forth wildly. Then, above the shoe, a teetery, tottery top hat appeared, and below the hat, a big red clown nose. The girls looked at one another, puzzled.

Then—*boing!*—Emerson bounced into the playhouse. "I've been such a clown," she said. She lifted one of her feet in its enormous shoe and tried to put it in her mouth. "I've really put my foot in my mouth, haven't I?" she said.

The girls had to giggle. Emerson looked so funny in her top hat, clown nose, and clown shoes!

Emerson held on to the brim of her hat and bowed. "I'm sorry. I hope we can start over." She pulled a rubber chicken out of her suitcase and waved it in the air, saying, "So, if anyone has an idea to share, don't be chicken!"

From under her hat, Emerson began
to pull what appeared to be an endless
sheet of paper. "I've got some ideas
right off the top of my head," she said.
She waggled one giant shoe in the air,
saying, "But this time, I want to get off
on the right foot, so I promise to listen
to your ideas first."

"Hooray!" cheered Emerson's
friends, laughing. They rushed toward
her, and soon she was in the middle of
a wildly wonderful WellieWisher hug.

Willa spoke up. "I have an idea," she said. "I've thought of a better way to sing the muddily-puddily song."

Then everyone began talking at once, bursting with good ideas. Soon, they were ready to put on their show. They invited Aunt Miranda and their friends and families to come see it the next day.

come to our
FALL
SHOW

Kendall and Camille were the first act in the show. They tossed leaves all over the stage as they sang to the tune of "London Bridge Is Falling Down":

Autumn leaves are falling down,
falling down, falling down.
Autumn leaves are falling down,
Oh, so pretty!

The audience clapped. Kendall and
Camille bowed, and Kendall ran off
the stage.

Ashlyn came onstage. Camille held up props while Ashlyn recited the "Yellow" poem.

Leaves are yellow
as a ripe banana,
Yellow as some cheese,
Yellow as the stripes
on the bumblebees!

Ashlyn and Camille bowed and left. Emerson came swirling in, dancing and spinning as she recited her poem.

Windy, windy
blue-sky day,
Swirl me up and
blow me away.

For the last act, Willa held up a big umbrella, and all the WellieWishers crowded in under it. They sang together to the tune of "Row, Row, Row Your Boat":

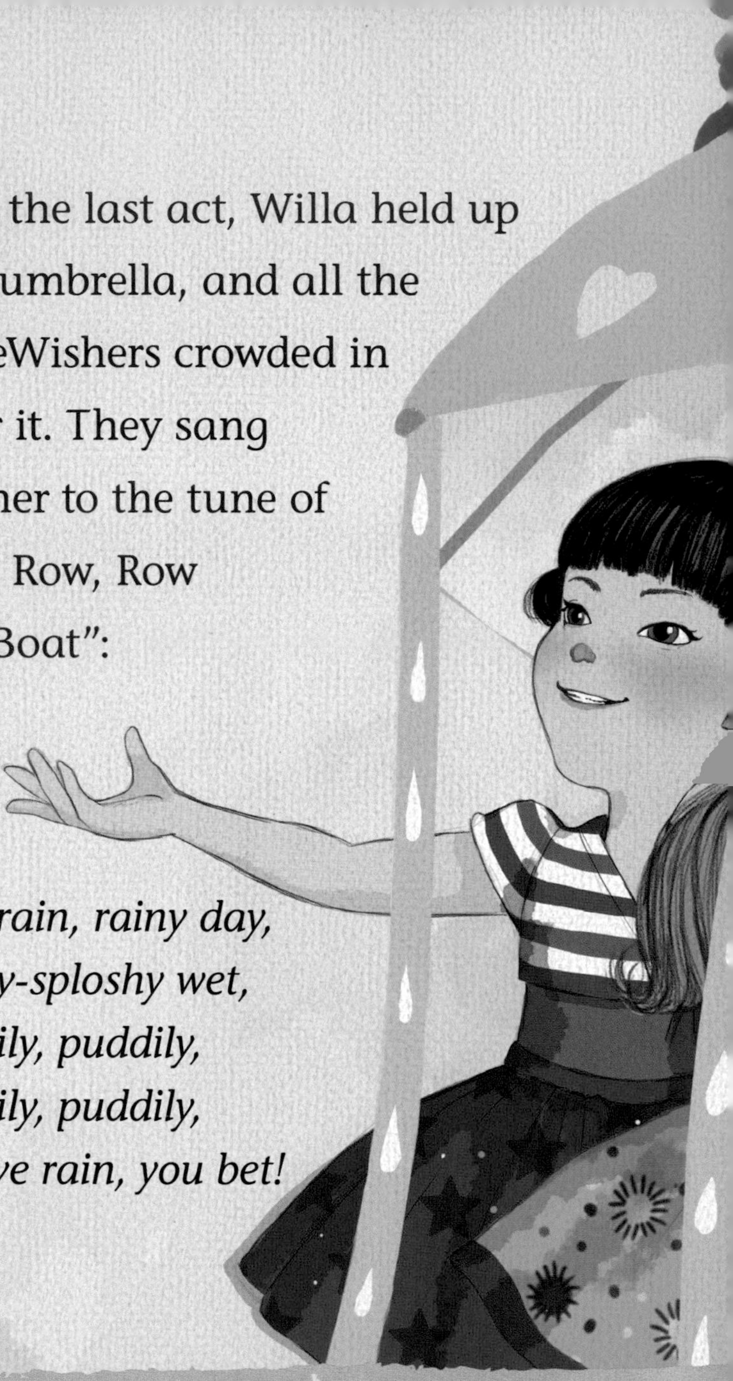

Rain, rain, rainy day,
Splishy-sploshy wet,
Muddily, puddily,
Muddily, puddily,
We love rain, you bet!

After the song, Emerson stepped forward. "Thank you for coming to our show," she said to the audience.

"Hooray!" shouted the audience. The WellieWishers took a bow as the audience clapped and whistled and cheered. "Hooray for the WellieWishers! Bravo!"

After the audience left, the WellieWishers sat on the stage together.

"Our 'Fall for Fall' show wasn't at all the way that I'd imagined it would be," said Emerson. She jumped up and spun on one toe. "It was better!"

And all the WellieWishers cheered, "Hooray for Emerson! Bravo!"

Managing Strong Emotions

Excitement is infectious, and there's nothing like a child bubbling over with big ideas! Sometimes, though, kids can get so carried away with enthusiasm that they don't realize not everyone shares their feelings. If your girl is feeling is out of sync with her friends, here are some ways to help her handle it.

❀ **Take a familiar song and rewrite the lyrics** to fit the situation. For example, if she's feeling frustrated, suggest that she finish these lines to the tune of "Twinkle, Twinkle, Little Star":

"I wish I knew how to _____

If I could, I'd _____ *."*

If the lines come out sounding funny or silly, so much the better! Music and humor are time-honored ways of gaining control over difficult feelings.

Creative Encouragement

If her friends are doing something that she finds difficult or daunting, remind her of things she has gotten better at over time, such as putting together puzzles or riding a bike. Praise her, and point out that other things will get easier as she gets older and has more practice. Offer to make a video of her doing something she's good at, then watch it together. Or try these simple crafts:

❀ **Help her draw a "talent tree"** on poster board. Identify her talents and talents-to-be by brainstorming all the activities she enjoys or is interested in. Help her write the activities on paper leaves and tape them to the tree, putting those she does well at the top and those she wants to work on lower on the tree. As she gets better at those things, she can move them up the tree!

Talent tree

writing
drawing
math
sports
puzzles
games
crafts

✿ **Help her make a scrapbook** of photos, school certificates, and notes from teachers and child-care providers highlighting her accomplishments. Every so often, look through it with her and talk about how much she has done. Keep adding to it!

✿ **Remind her that every girl has different strengths** and weaknesses, and ask her what she's most proud of in her own life. Help her make a top ten list and hang it in her room.

My top 10
1 Fast reader
2 Good friend
3 Helpful
4 Graceful
5 Creative
6
7

Boredom Busters

If she's got several friends over but they're growing bored or crabby, help her brainstorm alternative activities. These could be as simple as watching a movie, playing at the park, or doing a puzzle together. Or get a game going:

❊ **In the Manner of the Adverb:** One girl leaves the room. The other girls pick an adverb—a word ending in "ly" that describes the manner of an action, such as "quickly" or "crazily." The first girl returns and asks the girls to do something "in the manner of the adverb"—for example, "get dressed in the manner of the adverb." One at a time girls then act out their assignments—such as getting dressed super fast if the word is quickly, or saying "I think I'll wear my pants on my head" if the word is crazily. Unlike charades, talking is encouraged! When the adverb is guessed, the girl whose acting gave it away gets to go out, and the game continues.

❋ **Mirror Game:** Have the girls stand in front of a mirror and frown at their reflections. Now smile. Then frown again. Then smile really big. Then scowl fiercely. Keep going, with ever bigger expressions, faster and faster. This game usually ends in laughter!

About the Author

VALERIE TRIPP says that she became
a writer because of the kind of person she is.
She says she's curious, and writing requires you
to be interested in everything. Talking is her
favorite sport, and writing is a way of talking
on paper. She's a daydreamer, which helps her
come up with her ideas. And she loves words.
She even loves the struggle to come up
with just the right words as she writes
and rewrites. Ms. Tripp lives in
Maryland with her husband.